OUTDOOR EXPLORER

I SEE LEAVES

by Tim Mayerling

TABLE OF CONTENTS

tadpole books

I SEE LEAVES

Look at the leaves.

They are long and thin.

Look at the leaves.

They have many lobes.

Look at the leaves.

They look like a heart.

Look at the leaves.

They have pointed ends.

Look at the leaves.

They look like a fan.

Look at the leaves.

They have jagged edges.

Look at the leaves.

What shapes do you see?

WORDS TO KNOW

fan

heart

jagged

leaves

lobes

pointed

INDEX